A Tadpole Grows Up

Annabelle Gold

INFOMAX COMMON CORE READERS

Rosen Classroom™

New York

Published in 2013 by The Rosen Publishing Group, Inc.
29 East 21st Street, New York, NY 10010

Book Design: Michael Harmon

Photo Credits: Cover Dr. Morley Read/Shutterstock.com; p. 4 (frog) ponsuwan/Shutterstock.com;
pp. 4 (tadpole), 17 Turchina Natalia/Shutterstock.com; p. 5 DJTaylor/Shutterstock.com; p. 6 TTphoto/Shutterstock.
com; p. 7 Sefan Fierros/Shutterstock.com; p. 8 PRILL Mediendesign und Fotografie/Shutterstock.com; p. 9 knin/
Shutterstock.com; p. 10 bluecrayola/Shutterstock.com; p. 11 Sergey Toronto/Shutterstock.com; p. 12 koko-tewan/
Shutterstock.com; p. 13 Hugo Willcox/Foto Natura/Minden Pictures/Getty Images; p. 14 Dr. Morley Read/
Shutterstock.com; p. 15 © iStockphoto.com/DusanBartolovic; p. 16 Maxim Tupikov/Shutterstock.com;
p. 18 (frog on land) Hintau Aliaksei/Shutterstock.com; p. 18 (frog in water) ivaskes/Shutterstock.com; p. 19 Cathy
Keifer/Shutterstock.com; p. 20 F Millington/Taxi/Getty Images; p. 21 (frog) Frank Greenaway/Dorling Kindersley/Getty
Images; p. 21 (tadpoles) Helen Greenwood/Flickr/Getty Images.

ISBN: 978-1-4488-8983-9
6-pack ISBN: 978-1-4488-8984-6

Manufactured in the United States of America

CPSIA Compliance Information: Batch #WS12RC: For further information contact Rosen Publishing, New York, New York at 1-800-237-9932.

Word Count: 195

Contents

A tadpole is a baby frog.

Tadpoles come from eggs.

A mother frog lays her eggs in water.

Frog eggs are covered by a kind of jelly.

This keeps them safe.

The eggs stick together and float in water.

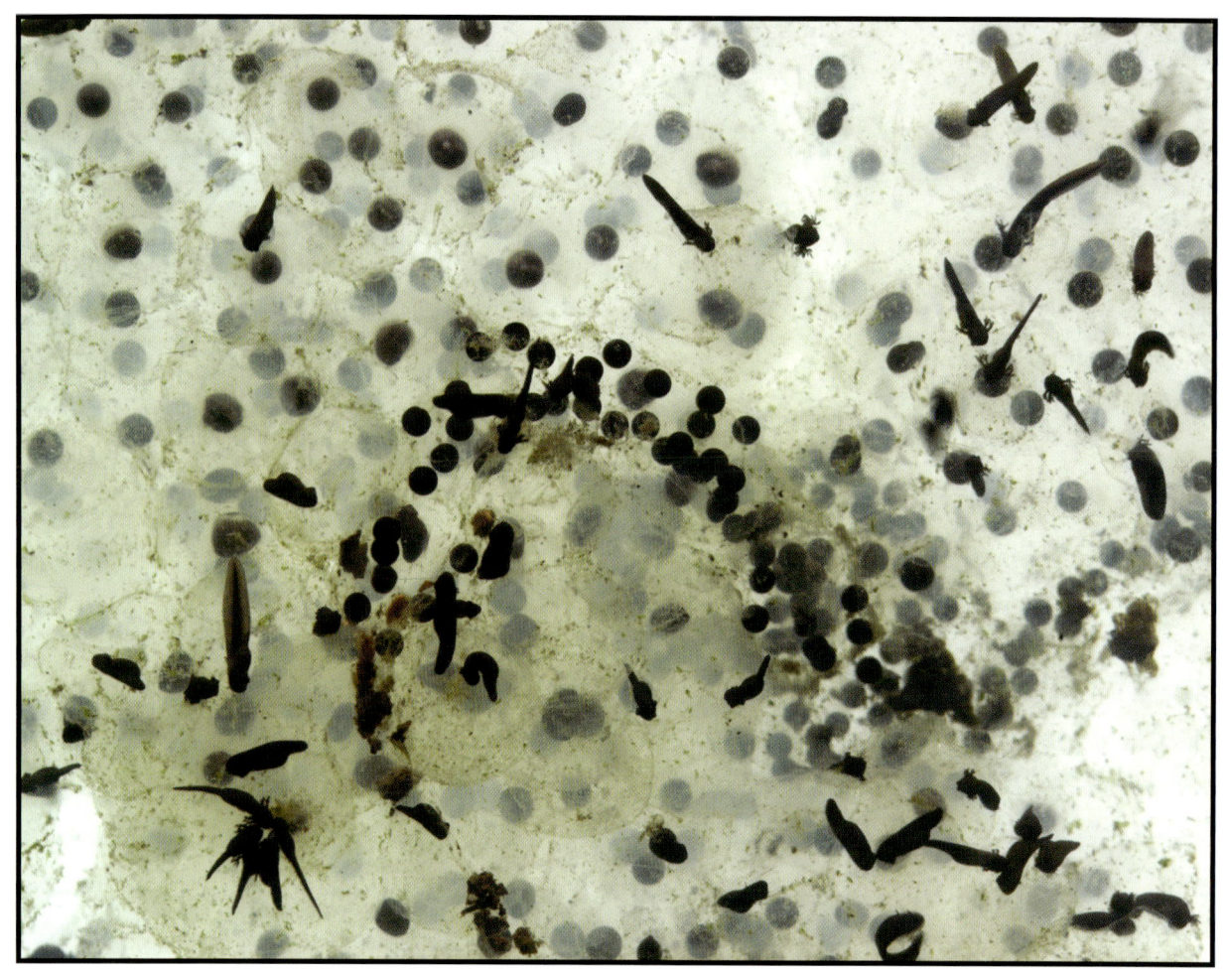

Then, a tadpole comes out of each egg.

A tadpole lives in the water.

It doesn't have legs, but it has a tail.

Tadpoles can swim and breathe
under the water.

Tadpoles eat small plants
that grow in water.

Soon, a tadpole starts to grow legs
so it can walk on land.

First, a tadpole grows two back legs.

Then, a tadpole grows two front legs.

It doesn't need its tail anymore.

Soon, a tadpole looks like a little frog.

It's called a froglet.

A froglet can swim to the top of the water because it can breathe air.

Then, a froglet becomes a young frog.

It has four legs and no tail.

A frog can live in the water or on land.

A frog eats bugs and worms!

When a frog is done growing,

it's called an adult.

A mother frog lays new eggs.

Soon, new tadpoles are born
and grow up to become frogs!

A Tadpole's Life

egg

tadpole

froglet

young frog

frog

Words to Know

froglet

jelly

tadpole

Index